Hesperidium

A young man finds a tree with strange fruit growing from it , looking almost like an orange but with dark purple skin and red flesh. The taste is extremely delicious and intoxicating , so then he collects all the fruit from this tree , hoping to keep some for himself and sell the rest of them.

'Paulette Tavormina'

~ A hesperidium is a septate fleshy fruit with a thick-skinned, leathery outer pericarp wall and fleshy modified trichomes {juice sacs} arising from the inner walls, as in Citrus {orange, lemon, grapefruit, etc.}

Notes On Shakespearean English ~

Shakespearean English, also known as Early Modern English, is the form of English used by William Shakespeare and others during the late 16th and early 17th centuries. It has distinct features compared to

Modern English, including different verb conjugations, vocabulary, and pronoun usage. While many words and phrases from Shakespeare's plays are still used today, there are also significant differences in language structure and style.

The most notable difference from modern English is the use of "thou" as the second-person singular pronoun, replaced by "you" in modern English. This also affects verb conjugations, such as "thou art'" or "thou dost".

'Where we add an –s to verbs, such as lives, builds, makes and believes, speakers added –eth:
Liveth = lives
Builders = builds
Believeth = believes

The most common verb is doth, which means does: The language doth confuse, yet she seeketh to understand, for understanding bringeth joy.

Similarly, dost means do.

Dost thou follow? Surely, thou dost understand!

He does = he doth.

You do = thou dost.

If you switch the sentence around, you would just add the –est to the verb:Surely, thou followest the pattern!' Wonderful! ~ 'https://shakespearenerd.home.blog/'

	Subject	Object	Dependent Possessive	Independent Possessive	Reflexive
First Person	I	me	my	mine	myself
Second Person (formal)	you	you	your	yours	yourself
Second Person (informal)	thou	thee	thy	thine	thyself
Third Person (masculine)	she	her	her	hers	herself
Third Person (feminine)	he	him	his	his	himself
Third person (gender neutral)	they	them	their	theirs	themself

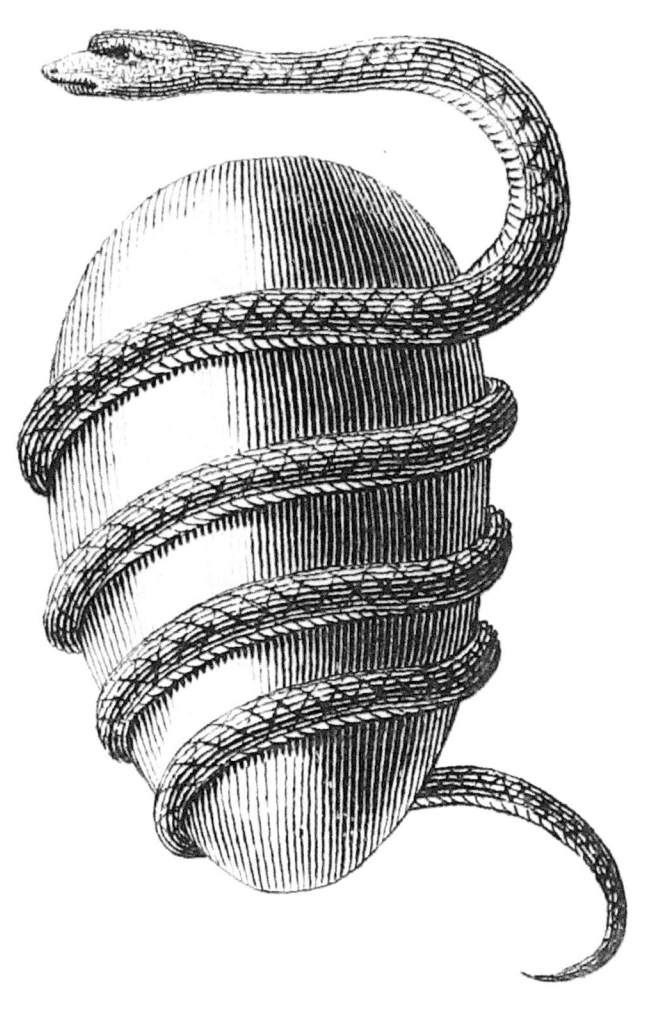

'*Jacob Bryant's Orphic Egg (1774)*'

'Theodor Mattenheimer ~ Still life with flowers and insects'

The forest breathed around Elias, a living entity of whispering leaves and rustling undergrowth. Sunlight, fractured by the dense green canopy, dappled the moist forest floor in an ethereal dance of light and shadow. He moved with a practiced grace, his tall, slender frame navigating the tangled roots and fallen branches with ease. His curly blonde hair, usually a riotous halo in the sun, was subdued beneath the shade of the large ancient trees, and his green eyes, sharp and observant, scanned the surroundings with a quiet intensity.

Elias was a child of the woods, more comfortable amongst the ancient trees than within the confines of the small village nestled at its edge. He knew the secrets of the forest intimately , the best places to find wild berries, the particular herbs his mother favored for her cooking, the hidden springs where the water ran purest. Today, his mission was simple: gather enough nettles , berries and dandelion roots to make a medicinal tea. Winter was coming soon , along with all its treacherous ailments.

He hummed a tuneless melody as he worked, his fingers nimble as they plucked the dark berries from their branches. The forest floor was a carpet of decay, rich with the scent of damp earth and decaying leaves. It was a scent he found comforting, a reminder of the cyclical nature of life and death, of growth and destruction. He was lost in the rhythm of his task when he noticed something unusual.

He had ventured further than he typically did, drawn by the promise of a particularly bountiful patch of berries. Now, standing in a small clearing bathed in an eerie twilight, he saw a tree unlike any he had ever encountered before. Its ragged bark was a deep, almost black hue, a stark contrast to the lighter shades of the surrounding trees. It was gnarled and twisted, its branches reaching out like skeletal fingers pointing towards the slowly fading sky. The air around it felt heavy, charged with a strange energy that made the hairs on the back of his neck prickle.

But it wasn't the tree's ominous appearance that truly captured his attention. Hanging from its branches, scattered amongst the dark leaves, were fruits unlike any he had ever seen. They were round, about the size of an orange, but their skin was a deep, unsettling purple. They seemed to glow faintly in the dim light, emanating a subtle, almost imperceptible hum.

Curiosity, a trait that often led the young boy into trouble, overwhelmed his heightened senses. He cautiously approached the tree, on high alert. The air grew colder as he neared, and the silence, usually broken by the chirping of birds or the rustling of leaves, became absolute silence, not a single bird stirred. He reached out a tentative hand and plucked one of the purple fruits from its thin , bony branch.

It felt strangely heavy in his muddy moss stained palm, the skin smooth and cool to the touch. It pulsed with a faint, internal light, as if alive with some unknown energy. He examined it closely, turning it over and over in his hands. It was perfect, flawless, yet undeniably unsettling.

He knew he shouldn't. Instinct screamed at him to drop the fruit and run, to put as much distance as possible between himself and this strange, unnatural tree. But the allure of the unknown was too strong to resist. He had to know what lay within.

With a deep breath, he dug his fingernail into the fruit's skin and began to peel it away. The skin came off easily, revealing a flesh that was even more startling than its exterior. It was a deep, vibrant red, the color of blood freshly spilled. He inhaled, expecting a familiar citrus scent, but instead, he was met with a subtle, almost floral aroma that made his stomach warm.

He hesitated, his hand trembling slightly. He knew nothing about this fruit, about its origins or its properties. It could be poisonous, deadly even. But the temptation, the insatiable desire to understand, to experience something new, was too powerful to ignore.

He broke the fruit open, revealing its core. It was a solid mass of the same deep red flesh, without a single seed in sight. It was unlike any fruit he had ever seen, defying the natural order, a bizarre anomaly in the heart of the woods.

He brought it closer to his nose, cautiously inhaling its strange, floral scent. He could almost taste it on his tongue, a sensation both intriguing and repulsive. He knew he shouldn't eat it, that it was foolish, reckless even. But the pull, the irresistible urge to taste this forbidden fruit, was overwhelming.

He closed his pale green eyes and took a small bite.

The taste was unlike anything he had ever experienced. It was sweet, almost cloyingly so, but with a sharp, metallic tang that lingered on his tongue. It was both delicious and disgusting, a paradoxical combination that sent shivers down his spine.

As he chewed, a strange sensation washed over him. His senses sharpened, the colors of the forest becoming more vibrant, the sounds of the woods amplified. He felt a surge of energy coursing through his veins, a feeling of invincibility, of boundless power that he had never felt before.

He swallowed, and the sensation intensified. He felt lighter, faster, stronger. He could hear the rustling of the leaves on the trees miles away, and see the tiny insects crawling on the forest floor. He felt connected to the forest in a way he had never experienced before, as if he had become a part of its very essence.

But then, the feeling began to change. The euphoria gave way to a creeping unease, a sense of dread that settled heavy in his stomach. The vibrant colors of the forest began to darken, the amplified sounds turning into a cacophony of noise that grated on his nerves.

He felt a coldness seeping into his bones, a chilling presence that seemed to emanate from the tree itself. He looked up at its gnarled branches, it's dark leaves rustling in the wind, and he saw something he hadn't noticed before.

Birds.

Hidden amongst the leaves, staring down at him with an unnerving intensity, were dozens of bird carcasses , they seemed to have no blood or organs contained in their lifeless bodies.

Panic surged through him. He dropped the remaining piece of the fruit, stumbled backwards, and turned to flee.

But it was too late.

His curiosity had taken complete hold of him.

The last rays of the setting sun bled across the forest, painting the gnarled branches of the old fruit trees in hues of crimson and gold. Elias, small for his fourteen years of age, moved with a practiced ease between the tree's branches, his bare feet sinking slightly into the soft earth. He hummed a tuneless melody as he reached for the fruit, his fingers brushing against the smooth, unfamiliar skin.

These were not the apples, pears, or plums that usually weighed down the branches of the village's trees. These were different.They felt heavy and cool in his hand, as if holding the secrets of the earth itself. He'd never seen fruit like this before, but the lure of their unusual beauty was irresistible.

The basket growing heavier with each carefully chosen piece, Elias felt a thrill course through him. He imagined his mother's surprise, the way her brow would furrow in that familiar, perplexed way. He pictured the villagers gathered around, their eyes wide with curiosity and perhaps, just a touch of envy.

These fruits could bring him and his mother out of poverty , if they sold them to their fellow villagers for a good price and kept the tree's exact whereabouts a complete secret.

As the last sliver of sun dipped below the horizon, casting long, menacing shadows across the orchard, Elias knew he had to leave. He hoisted the basket onto his shoulder, the weight digging into his thin frame, and he began to run. The path that led home was narrow and winding, snaking through the whispering fields of tall grass. Every rustle, every snap of a twig underfoot, sent a shiver down his spine. The tales of the forest, whispered by the elders in the village, were full of creatures that lurked in the darkness, creatures with eyes like burning coals and claws like razors.

He burst through the door of their small cottage, the familiar scent of woodsmoke and dried herbs filling his small fatigued lungs. His mother was hunched over the hearth, stirring a pot of something that smelled faintly of bitter roots and earthy mushrooms. Her face, etched with the lines of hardship and worry, lit up momentarily as she saw him.

"Elias! Wh're hast thee been? I hath sent thee out to gath'r nettles, dandelion roots and b'rries hours ago. The sun has already set!" Her voice, though laced with concern, held a sharp edge. Life in the village was hard, and every task, no matter how small, was crucial for survival.

Elias, breathless and flushed, set the basket down with a thud. "I know, Moth'r, but behold what I hath found!"

His mother straightened, her keen eyes scanning the contents of the basket. The firelight flickered across the strange, purple fruit, casting an eerie glow. Her expression shifted from annoyance to confusion. "What art these?" she asked, her voice laced with suspicion.

She reached into the basket, picking up one of the fruits and turning it over in her calloused hands.

"I know not," Elias admitted, his excitement undeterred. "I hath found them deep in the forest. Ive nev'r seen aught liketh these fruits bef're."

She examined the fruit more closely, sniffing it cautiously. The scent was sweet, but with an underlying note that she couldn't quite place. It was foreign, unfamiliar, and it made her uneasy. She had lived in this village her entire life, and she knew every tree, every plant, every berry that grew within its boundaries. These fruits were an anomaly.

"Wh're as ever did thee find these?" she asked, her voice low and serious.

"In the woods, Moth'r. On the far side."

Her grip tightened on the fruit. The far side of the forest was a place that most villagers avoided. It was said to be haunted by the spirits of those who had died during the great plague, their souls forever trapped among the gnarled branches and overgrown weeds.

"These... these come not from 'round here," she said, her voice barely a whisper. "Ive nev'r seen aught liketh them."

Elias, sensing her apprehension, reached out and plucked a fruit from her hand. "Just tryeth , Moth'r," he urged, his eyes shining with anticipation. "It tastes liketh naught thee has't ev'r tasted bef're."

She hesitated, her gaze flickering between the fruit and her son's eager face. Trusting her instincts was second nature to her, and her instincts were screaming at her to stay away. But she couldn't deny the genuine excitement in Elias's eyes, the hope that she would share in his discovery.

With a sigh, she raised the fruit to her lips and took a small bite. The taste exploded on her tongue, a symphony of sweetness and tartness, followed by a strange, almost metallic aftertaste. She closed her eyes, her senses overwhelmed. It was unlike anything she had ever experienced.

When she opened her eyes, her confusion had deepened. "Wh're... wh're did thee very much find this fruit, Elias? Where doth it come from?" she asked, her voice barely audible. "Tis not natural. Nothing like this grows in the village."

Elias, emboldened by her reaction, beamed. "I told thee, M'ther! It cometh from the forest. I can show you t'morrow."

She shook her head, her eyes fixed on the basket overflowing with the strange, purple fruit. A chill ran down her spine, a feeling of foreboding that settled deep in her bones.

"Nay," she said firmly. "Not tom'rrow. Tis almost nightfall. We shall speak of this in the m'rning."

She took the basket from him, placing it carefully on the floor in the corner of the cottage, as far away from the hearth as possible. "Wend to sleep now, Elias," she said, her voice softer now, but still laced with concern. "We shall speak of this in the m'rning."

Elias, disappointed that his mother didn't share his enthusiasm, nodded and retreated to his small sleeping pallet in the corner. He watched as his mother meticulously cleaned the pot by the fire, her movements stiff and deliberate. He knew she was worried, but he couldn't understand why. The fruit was beautiful, delicious, and unlike anything they had ever seen before. What was there to be afraid of?

As he drifted off to sleep, he dreamed of the forest, the trees laden with the strange, purple fruit, their branches whispering secrets in the wind. He dreamed of the faces of the villagers, their eyes wide with wonder as he presented them with his discovery.

But in his mother's mind, the fruit was casting a long, dark shadow. She couldn't shake the feeling that Elias had stumbled upon something dangerous, something that was not meant to be found. She knew that she had to find out where this fruit came from, and she knew that she had to protect her son from whatever secrets it held. The night was long, and filled with the rustling sounds of the forest, each sound amplifying her growing unease. She knew, with a certainty that chilled her to the core, that the discovery of the strange, purple fruit had changed something, and that their lives would never be the same again.

'Basket of Fruit ~ by Sina Irani'

The first awakening pains of nausea snaked around Elias's stomach even before he opened his eyes. A dull throbbing that pulsed behind his temples, a grim counterpoint to the chirping of the unseen birds outside his window. He lay still for a moment, hoping the feeling would pass, melt back into the shadows from whence it came. But it didn't. It only tightened its grip, a cold fist clenching deeper with each passing second.

He forced himself to sit up, the movement sending a fresh wave of dizziness through his entire body. The small, sparsely furnished room swam for a moment, the familiar outlines of the wooden dresser and the worn rug blurring into indistinct shapes. He clung to the edge of the bed, breathing deeply, until the world steadied itself again.

Whatever had been wrong, it felt like it had drained him of all his strength. He dragged himself out of bed, his legs heavy and unresponsive, and shuffled towards the door.

The smell of baking bread hit him as he descended the creaking stairs, a warm, yeasty aroma that usually brought a smile to his face. Today, it only served to intensify the queasiness churning in his gut. He stumbled into the kitchen, where his mother stood by the stove, her face etched with a worry that mirrored his own discomfort.

"Elias, thee look pale," she said, her voice laced with concern. She reached out and touched his forehead, her hand cool against his feverish skin. "Thou art burning up. What be wrong?"

He tried to smile reassuringly, but it felt like a grimace. "Just a did bite und'r the weath'r, Moth'r. Nothing to w'rry about."

She didn't look convinced. "Sit," she commanded, gesturing towards the worn wooden table. "I've made thee some broth and bread. Thee need something in thy stomach."

He sank onto the bench, the rough wood digging into his skin. The thought of food was the last thing he wanted, but he knew better than to argue with his mother when she was in her nurturing mode. She was strong, resourceful, a pillar of strength in their small, isolated existence. He owed it to her to at least try.

She placed a steaming bowl of broth in front of him, its savory scent threatening to overwhelm him all over again. The bread, still warm from the oven, sat beside it, its crust a deep, inviting brown. He picked up the spoon, his hand trembling slightly, and took a tentative sip.

The broth was surprisingly soothing, a rich, complex flavor that slowly unfurled on his tongue. It was made with herbs from her garden and bones she had saved from last week's roast, a concoction she claimed could cure anything short of death itself. He took another sip, and then another, the warmth spreading through him, chasing away the chill that had settled in his bones.

He broke off a piece of the bread and dipped it into the broth, the soft, yielding texture a welcome contrast to the churning in his stomach. The bread was slightly sweet, almost nutty from the grains his mother ground herself. He ate slowly, savoring each mouthful, as if trying to coax his body back to life.

His mother watched him, her eyes filled with a quiet vigilance. She didn't speak, didn't press him to eat more than he could manage. She simply sat beside him, her presence a comforting anchor in the storm that raged within him.

As he ate, the nausea began to recede, replaced by a fragile sense of well being. The throbbing in his head lessened, and the world seemed to sharpen into focus. The colors in the room became brighter, the sounds of the morning more distinct.

By the time he finished the bowl of broth and the last piece of bread, he felt almost human again. He pushed the bowl away and leaned back against the bench, his body finally relaxing.

"Thanketh thee, Moth'r," he said, his voice still a little raspy. "It did bestow very much help."

She smiled, a genuine, heartfelt smile that reached her eyes. "I'm fain. You hadst me w'rri'd there f'r a moment."

He stood up, feeling a surge of energy he hadn't felt all morning. "I shall wend check on the animals," he said. "Those lot perchance haven't been fed aught yet."

His mother nodded. "Beest careful," she cautioned. "Ov'rdo not."

He stepped out into the yard, the cool morning air a welcome balm against his skin. The sun was higher now, bathing the world in a golden light. He took a deep breath, the scent of earth and animals filling his lungs. The farmyard, usually a source of endless chores, now seemed oddly comforting, a familiar space where he belonged.

The goats greeted him with bleating enthusiasm, their eager eyes fixed on the empty feed troughs. The pigs grunted and jostled each other in their pen, their snouts twitching with anticipation. He grabbed a pitchfork and began to clean out the pens, the familiar rhythm of the work grounding him, pushing the last vestiges of his illness away.

He shoveled manure, scattered fresh straw, and filled the feed troughs with grain. The work was hard, tiring, but he welcomed the physical exertion. It was a way to prove to himself that he was still strong, still capable, still the Elias his mother knew and relied on.

As he worked, he noticed a small, dark patch of mud near the pigpen, something he hadn't seen before. He frowned, his brow furrowing in concentration. It was too dark to be regular mud, almost black, and it seemed to have a strange, oily sheen.

He poked it with the pitchfork, breaking the surface. A faint, unpleasant odor wafted up, a smell he couldn't quite place. He recoiled instinctively, a shiver running down his spine.

Ignoring the feeling, he poked it more, and the mud gave way to reveal something else. Dark, oily and covered in dirt, was something almost akin to dried blood. This was when Elias stepped away and called his mother.

He knew in his gut that whatever this dark patch was, it wasn't natural, it wasn't right. It was a stain on the land, a shadow lurking beneath the surface of their peaceful existence. And he had a feeling, a growing certainty, that the nausea from this morning, the weakness, the strange scent in the air, were all connected to this dark and unsettling discovery. The peace of the morning vanished, leaving only the cold dread of the unknown.

'Still life with Fruit on a Stone Ledge by MARIA MARGITSON - Cambridge Fine Art'

The air in the forest was thick with the scent of damp earth and decaying leaves, a familiar perfume that usually calmed Elias. But today, a prickle of unease crawled beneath his skin, a disquiet he couldn't quite name. He walked with a measured pace, the gnarled roots of ancient trees clawing at the path, each step echoing in the hushed stillness. He was headed back to the fruit tree, the one he had stumbled upon a day ago.

The memory of that first encounter was still vivid. He had been lost, hopelessly turned around after venturing deeper into the woods than he usually dared. Then, like a beacon, he had seen it – a tree laden with fruit unlike any he had ever seen before. They were plump and round, with a skin that shimmered with an almost ethereal glow, a deep crimson that bled into hints of gold at their stems. The taste had been extraordinary, a burst of sweetness that lingered on his tongue, leaving him feeling invigorated and strangely... connected.

He had taken only a few, enough to satisfy his immediate hunger and to bring back for his mother. She had been as captivated by the fruit as he was, devouring it in secret whilst he slept.

As he approached the familiar clearing, his pace quickened. The tree stood bathed in the dappled sunlight, its branches reaching towards the sky like supplicating arms. He noticed immediately that it was even more laden with fruit than before. More of the crimson orbs pulsed with vibrant color, seemingly thriving in the secluded sanctuary. A smile tugged at the corner of his lips. He could gather enough to last them for days, maybe even weeks.

He reached out, his fingers brushing against the smooth skin of a particularly tempting fruit. It felt warm to the touch, almost alive. He plucked it gently from the branch, admiring its perfect form. As he did, a twig snapped behind him.

Elias froze, his senses on high alert. The forest held its breath, the usual symphony of rustling leaves and chirping birds silenced. He slowly turned, his heart hammering against his ribs.

Standing at the edge of the clearing, bathed in shadow, was a deer. But this was no ordinary deer. Its eyes, usually soft and gentle, burned with an unsettling intensity, a dark, almost malevolent glint. Its antlers, thick and gnarled, were not the velvety brown he was used to seeing, but a stark, bone white that seemed to radiate a chilling aura.

Elias had encountered deer in the forest before. They were usually skittish creatures, quick to flee at the first sign of human presence. But this one stood its ground, its gaze unwavering, fixed solely on him.

A low growl rumbled from the deer's throat, a sound that sent a shiver down Elias's spine. It lowered its head, its antlers pointing directly at him. He knew, with a sudden, terrifying certainty, that this was not a friendly encounter.

Adrenaline surged through his veins. He dropped the fruit, its crimson surface rolling on the mossy ground. He knew he had to run.

The deer charged.

Elias didn't hesitate. He turned and bolted, his legs pumping, his lungs burning. The sound of the deer's hooves pounding against the earth echoed behind him, growing closer with each stride. He glanced back over his shoulder and saw, to his horror, that the deer was gaining on him. Its eyes were wild, its antlers lowered, a weapon poised to strike.

He plunged deeper into the woods, weaving between the trees, desperately trying to put distance between himself and the pursuing creature. Thorns tore at his clothes, branches whipped at his face, but he didn't dare slow down. He could feel the hot breath of the deer on his neck, the ground vibrating with its relentless pursuit.

He stumbled, tripping over a gnarled root, and landed hard on the forest floor. Pain shot through his ankle, but he forced himself to his feet, ignoring the throbbing ache. He knew that if he stayed down, even for a moment, it would be over.

He scrambled up a steep incline, clawing at the earth for purchase. The deer was right behind him, its snorting breath a terrifying accompaniment to his own ragged gasps. He reached the top of the rise and saw, to his relief, a dense thicket of thorny bushes. It was his only chance.

He dove into the thicket, the thorns tearing at his skin, ripping his clothes. He pushed through, ignoring the pain, knowing that the deer wouldn't follow. It was too large, its antlers too wide to navigate the dense undergrowth.

He collapsed on the other side, gasping for breath, his body trembling with exhaustion and fear. He could hear the deer pacing back and forth on the other side of the thicket, its frustrated snorts echoing through the woods. He stayed there, hidden and motionless, for what felt like an eternity, until finally, the sounds faded away.

Slowly, cautiously, he emerged from the thicket, his body a patchwork of scratches and bruises. He looked back towards the clearing, towards the tree laden with its tempting fruit. It seemed to glisten in the sunlight, an innocent beacon in the now menacing landscape.

But he knew, with a chilling certainty, that it was no longer safe. The forest, once a place of wonder and solace, had revealed a darker side, a hidden malevolence that he couldn't ignore. The deer, with its burning eyes and bone white antlers, was a guardian, a protector of something he didn't understand.

He turned and walked away, away from the fruit tree, away from the clearing, away from the darkness that had taken root in the woods. He limped, his ankle throbbing with pain, but he didn't stop.

He returned home, his heart heavy with fear and regret. He didn't tell his mother what had happened, not wanting to frighten her. He simply said that he hadn't been able to find any more fruit. She looked at him with a mixture of disappointment and concern, but she didn't press him.

That night, he lay awake, staring at the ceiling, the image of the deer seared into his mind. He knew that he would never forget the encounter, the chilling intensity of its gaze, the terrifying certainty of its intent. He knew that something had shifted in the forest, a balance had been disturbed, and he had been caught in the middle.

He wondered what the fruit was, what power it held, and why the deer was so determined to protect it. He knew that he would probably never know the answers, but he also knew that he had learned a valuable lesson. Some things are best left undisturbed, some mysteries are best left unsolved.

The forest, he realized, held secrets that were not meant for human eyes, and some doors, once opened, could never be closed again. He had glimpsed a darkness that lay hidden beneath the surface of the natural world, and he knew that he would carry that knowledge with him always. He had gone seeking sweetness, but he had found something far more bitter, a taste of the wild, untamed heart of the woods. And he knew, with a deep and unsettling certainty, that he would never be the same again.

'Rachel Ruysch ~ Fruit and Insects'

A cold slither of awareness snaked through Elias's mind, bringing with them the familiar, unwelcome guest: nausea. It was a thick, cloying feeling that coated his tongue and churned in the pit of his stomach, a constant companion these last few weeks. He groaned, turning onto his side, his hand instinctively going to his abdomen. It offered no comfort.

He opened his eyes, the dim morning light filtering through the cracks in the boarded up window doing little to alleviate the gloom of the small room. The air was thick with the smell of damp earth and something vaguely metallic, a scent he'd grown accustomed to in this forsaken place. He squeezed his eyes shut again, willing the nausea to subside, but it persisted, a dull, throbbing ache that made him want to curl up and disappear.

With a sigh, Elias pushed himself up, the meager blanket sliding off his shoulders. The floorboards creaked under his bare feet as he made his way to the small, makeshift table in the corner. Breakfast. He knew he needed to eat, even if the thought made his stomach recoil. He had to keep his strength up, even if he felt like he was constantly fighting a losing battle.

On the table sat a crust of stale bread, a bowl of thin, watery soup, and a handful of unfamiliar, brightly colored fruit. The bread looked unappetizing, dry and hard, but he tore off a piece and chewed it slowly, forcing it down. The soup was a little better, bland and almost tasteless, but at least it was liquid. He swallowed it, a few spoonfuls at a time, trying not to focus on the way his stomach protested.

Then there was the fruit. It was new, brought to him by his mother. She must have searched for the tree and indeed found it. She hadn't spoken a word, just silently deposited the basket and disappeared back into the trees.He picked one up, the skin smooth and cool against his fingertips. It smelled sweet, almost intoxicatingly so.

He took a bite. For a moment, the nausea receded, replaced by a fleeting sensation of something akin to pleasure. He ate another, and then another, until only a few remained.

He finished the last of the fruit, hoping that it would settle his stomach, provide some relief. He waited, but the nausea returned, stronger this time, a wave of dizziness washing over him. He stumbled back to the bed, his hand flying to his mouth. He swallowed hard, fighting the urge to vomit.

The room began to spin. He sank onto the edge of the bed, his head in his hands. The sweet taste of the fruit turned sour in his mouth, a mocking reminder of the brief reprieve it had offered. He had hoped, foolishly, that it would be a cure, a solution to the sickness that plagued him. But it had only made things worse.

He lay back down, pulling the blanket over him, his body trembling. He closed his eyes, trying to block out the swirling sensations, the relentless nausea. He needed to rest, to heal. But sleep was elusive, haunted by the creeping fear that gnawed at the edges of his mind.

What was happening to him? He had been strong, healthy just a few months ago. Now, he was weak, constantly sick, trapped in this desolate place. He had no idea how he had gotten here, no memory of the events that had led him to this isolated room in the middle of nowhere. His memories were fragmented, like shards of glass, sharp and painful to touch. The details were hazy, obscured by a fog of confusion and terror.

And then there was the sickness. It wasn't just nausea; it was a deep, pervasive feeling of wrongness, as if something inside him was slowly twisting, corrupting him from the inside out. He could feel it in his bones, in his blood, a cold, creeping dread that seeped into his very soul.

He spent the day drifting in and out of consciousness, the nausea a constant, oppressive weight. The sun climbed higher in the sky, casting long, distorted shadows across the room. He tried to distract himself, to focus on anything other than the sickness, but his thoughts kept returning to the same questions. Who was he? Why was he here? And what was happening to him?

He tried to remember something, anything, that could offer a clue.

THE FRUIT

The strange , foreign hesperidium that he had came across deep in the forest. *I shall never touch that fruit again* he thought knowing he most likely couldn't make such a promise to himself.

As evening approached, the nausea began to subside, replaced by a bone-deep exhaustion. He knew he needed to eat again, but the thought of food made his stomach churn. He forced himself to sit up, his body aching. He needed to find something, anything, to sustain him.

He stumbled to the table, his hand brushing against the empty bowl that had held the fruit. The sweet smell lingered in the air, a faint, almost mocking reminder of the brief relief it had provided. He stared at the bowl, his mind racing.

THE FRUIT

He shuddered, the thought sending a chill down his spine. He didn't want to believe it, but the evidence was mounting. He couldn't ignore the way the nausea had intensified after he had eaten the fruit. He couldn't ignore the feeling that something was fundamentally wrong.

He pushed the bowl away, his stomach clenching. He would not eat any more of the fruit. He would starve first.

With a sigh, he sank back onto the bed, the darkness closing in around him. He knew he was alone, trapped in this forsaken place with a sickness he didn't understand and memories he couldn't grasp. He was lost, adrift in a sea of uncertainty and fear.

But even in the depths of despair, a flicker of defiance remained. He would not give up. He would fight, even if he didn't know what he was fighting for. He would survive, somehow, even if it meant facing the darkness alone.

'Still Life with Fruits – Museum of Fine Arts, Budapest'

The darkness in Elias's small room was a thick, suffocating blanket, woven with the threads of exhaustion and the ever present chill of the stone walls. He had finally drifted into a restless sleep, the day's toil still clinging to him like cobwebs. The rhythmic creaks and groans of the ancient house, usually a comforting lullaby, were tonight punctuated by something far more jarring.

A harsh, rattling cough tore through the silence. Elias bolted upright, his heart hammering against his ribs. It was his mother. Her cough was a raw, ragged sound, like dry leaves being crushed underfoot, a sound that had become increasingly familiar in the long, bleak winter.

He fumbled for the flint and steel on his bedside table, his fingers clumsy with sleep. Sparks flew, catching on the tinder, and within moments, a small, flickering flame danced at the tip of the candle. He shielded it with his hand, the weak light casting elongated, distorted shadows across the room.

Elias rose, his bare feet cold against the stone floor. The chill seeped into his bones, a constant reminder of the harshness of their existence. He held the candle aloft, its small sphere of light pushing back the darkness as he crept towards the door.

His mother's room was at the end of a narrow corridor, each step echoing in the oppressive silence. The coughing continued, a relentless, agonizing spasm that wracked her frail body. With each cough, a fresh wave of fear washed over Elias, cold and heavy.

He reached her door, his hand hovering over the latch for a moment. He hesitated, torn between the desire to rush to her side and the ingrained habit of respecting her privacy. But the cough, growing ever more desperate, decided for him. He pushed the door open gently, the hinges groaning in protest.

The room was dimly lit by the embers in the hearth, casting dancing shadows on the walls. His mother lay in the large, four-poster bed, propped up by a mountain of pillows. Her face, usually etched with a quiet strength, was pale and drawn, her eyes shadowed with fatigue. She coughed again, a deep, wrenching sound that left her breathless.

"Moth'r?" Elias whispered, his voice barely audible above the crackling of the fire. He moved closer, holding the candle high. "Art thee good now?"

She turned her head towards him, her eyes flickering with a weariness that mirrored his own. She raised a hand, her fingers thin and trembling, and offered a weak smile.

"Tis fine, Elias," she rasped, her voice hoarse and strained. "Go back to sleep. Tis just a tickle in my throat."

Her words were meant to reassure, but they did little to quell the fear that gnawed at him. He stood still , his gaze fixed upon her.

She waved a dismissive hand, her smile unwavering, though Elias could see the pain etched around her eyes. "Child. I'm just a dram bitter cold. A did bite of rest is all I need."

He stood there, his mind warring with itself. He wanted to believe her, to trust that she would be alright. But the cough, that relentless, hacking cough, told a different story.

"Can I recieveth thee aught, Moth'r?" he asked, his voice trembling slightly. "Some wat'r? Some tea?"

She shook her head. "Just wend back to sleep, Elias"

He knew she was trying to protect him, trying to shield him from the worry that was already consuming him. She always did. She had been both mother and father to him since he was a small boy, her strength and resilience a constant source of inspiration. But tonight, her usual fortitude seemed to falter, her words lacking their usual conviction.

He lingered for a moment longer, his eyes scanning her face, searching for any sign that she was truly alright. But all he saw was weariness and a desperate attempt to appear strong.

He backed out of the room slowly, his eyes fixed on her face until the darkness swallowed him. He closed the door gently, the click of the latch echoing in the silence.

He stood in the corridor for a long moment, listening to the ragged sound of her breathing. The coughing subsided slightly, but the silence that followed was just as unsettling. He knew he wouldn't be able to sleep.

He turned and walked back to his room, the candle flame flickering in the draft. He placed it on his bedside table and sat on the edge of the bed, his gaze fixed on the dancing flame.

He knew he should obey her, and should try to sleep. But he couldn't. He couldn't shake the feeling that something was terribly wrong. He couldn't ignore the fear that was clawing at his insides.

He rose again and moved to the window. He pushed back the heavy curtains and peered out into the darkness. The moon was a sliver in the sky, casting a pale, ethereal light on the snow-covered landscape. The wind howled through the trees, a mournful sound that seemed to mirror the despair in his heart.

He stood there for a long time, watching the swirling snow and listening to the wind. He felt utterly helpless, unable to do anything to ease his mother's suffering. He was just a boy, barely more than a child, burdened with the weight of the world.

He crept back to her room and listened at the door. The coughing had stopped, but he could hear her shallow, labored breathing. He hesitated for a moment, then gently pushed the door open.

The room was still dark, but he could see her lying in bed, her face pale and still. He moved closer, his heart pounding in his chest.

"Moth'r?" he whispered, his voice trembling. "Moth'r, art thee awake?"

She didn't respond.

He reached out and gently touched her hand. It was cold.

A wave of panic washed over him. He shook her gently. "Moth'r! Wake up!"

Still, she didn't stir.

He leaned closer, his ear near her mouth. He could hear her breathing, faint and shallow, but he couldn't feel her breath on his cheek.

He scrambled back, his mind reeling. His entire body filled with terror and grief.

But suddenly the woman's eyes opened 'What didst I bid thee knave! Wend back to sleep!'

He turned and ran from the room, his bare feet pounding on the stone floor.

The darkness that had haunted him throughout the night now seemed to cling to him, urging him to give up. But he pushed it back, fueled by a desperate hope.

'Still life of fruit and flowers ~Ashmolean Museum, Oxford'

The morning arrived draped in a somber gray, mirroring the weight in Elias's chest. He could hear his mother upstairs, her cough a ragged, painful sound that sliced through the silence of the old farmhouse. She was still sick. The fever hadn't broken, and the weakness clung to her like a second skin.

He knew he should wake her, try to coax her into drinking some water at least, but the thought of her pale face, the dark circles under her eyes, made his stomach clench. So, he lingered a moment longer in the shadow of the doorway, listening to the rhythm of her breathing, a fragile, unsteady beat in the quiet house.

Elias crept downstairs, his bare feet silent on the worn wooden planks. The kitchen was cold and still, the lingering scent of herbs from the forest were hanging in the air.

The iron stove was cold. He rummaged in the wood bin, his fingers brushing against rough bark, and began the arduous task of building a fire. The kindling crackled and popped, slowly coaxing the larger logs into flame. As the heat began to radiate, chasing away the chill, he found the pot of leftover vegetable soup in the pantry. It looked congealed and unappetizing, but with a little coaxing and a splash of water, he hoped he could make it palatable.

He placed the pot on the stove, stirring occasionally, his thoughts a swirling mix of hope and fear. He imagined his mother sitting up in bed, smiling weakly as she sipped the warm broth. He imagined the fever breaking, her strength returning, her laughter echoing through the house once more. But the images were fragile, easily shattered by the persistent cough that drifted down from upstairs.

As the soup warmed, a new scent began to permeate the air. It wasn't the comforting aroma of simmering vegetables, but something acrid and sickly sweet, something deeply unsettling. Elias frowned, sniffing the air, trying to pinpoint the source. It was a fleshy, decaying smell, like something left to rot in the sun.

He finally traced the odor to the gathering basket, a large woven container that usually sat near the back door. His mother had been going back to the forest and collecting the fruit.

Curiosity warred with a growing sense of unease. He hadn't looked in the basket for a few days, preoccupied with his mother's illness. But now, the stench was impossible to ignore.

He approached the basket cautiously, the horrible smell intensifying with each step. The woven reeds seemed to writhe in the dim light, taking on a sinister quality he hadn't noticed before. He hesitated, his hand hovering over the rim. Something felt wrong, deeply wrong.

Taking a deep breath, he reached down and grabbed the basket. It was surprisingly light. He lifted the old stained burlap cloth that covered the contents, expecting to find a few withered apples needing to be discarded.

What he saw made him recoil in horror.

Most of the fruit was gone. Vanished. But nestled at the bottom of the basket, amidst a pool of thick, dark liquid, were a handful of misshapen, rotting remnants. They were barely recognizable as apples and pears. Their skins were bruised and blackened, their flesh softened and pulpy. The juice, thick and viscous, oozed from their decaying forms like blood.

The smell was overwhelming, a nauseating blend of decay and fermentation. It clung to the back of his throat, making him gag. He stared, transfixed, at the grotesque display, his mind struggling to comprehend what he was seeing.

How could they have rotted so quickly? Now, they were reduced to this horrifying mess.

A shiver ran down his spine, a cold, primal fear that had nothing to do with the putrid smell or the decaying fruit. There was something unnatural about this, something…wrong.

His eyes scanned the basket again, searching for any clue, any explanation. He noticed a faint, glistening trail leading from the basket towards the back door. It was barely visible in the dim light, a thin, shimmering line that disappeared into the shadows.

He followed the trail, his heart pounding in his chest. It led him to the back door, which he was sure he had locked the night before. Now, it was slightly ajar, a sliver of gray light seeping into the kitchen.

He reached out, his hand trembling, and pushed the door open a crack. The cold air rushed in, carrying with it the scent of pine and damp earth. But beneath the familiar smells, he detected a faint, lingering trace of the same sickeningly sweet odor that emanated from the basket.

He peered out into the gray morning. The yard was empty, shrouded in mist. The skeletal branches of the apple trees clawed at the sky. But something felt different, wrong. He couldn't shake the feeling that he was being watched, that something was lurking just beyond the veil of mist.

He slammed the door shut, his breath coming in ragged gasps. He locked the bolt, the metallic click echoing in the silent kitchen. He backed away from the door, his eyes darting around the room, searching for any sign of danger.

The soup on the stove had begun to bubble, the gentle sound a stark contrast to the frantic beat of his heart. He blew off the heat, the smell of the soup now tainted by the lingering stench of decay. He couldn't bring himself to give it to his mother. Not now.

He returned to the basket, his gaze fixed on the rotting fruit. He had to get rid of it. He couldn't leave it in the house, poisoning the air, feeding whatever darkness had crept into their home.

He found a shovel in the shed and carefully scooped the decaying mess into it, the sticky juice clinging to the metal. He carried it far from the house, to the edge of the woods, and dumped it into a shallow pit. He covered it with earth and leaves, burying the horror beneath the cold, damp ground.

As he walked back to the house, the fear that had been simmering beneath the surface finally boiled over. His mother was sick, the harvest was rotting, and something was lurking in the shadows. He was alone, and he was terrified.

He knew, with a chilling certainty, that this was just the beginning. The horror had taken root in his home, and it wouldn't be easily banished. The decay had begun, and it threatened to consume everything he held dear. He had to find a way to stop it, before it was too late. But he had no idea where to begin. The darkness had already begun to creep in.

'Frans Snyders or Snijders - Still Life of Fruit on a Ledge'

The first scream tore through the veil of Elias's sleep like a jagged knife. It was a raw, animalistic sound, laced with terror that resonated deep within his bones. And it was his mother's voice. He shot up in bed, heart hammering against his ribs, the remnants of a peaceful dream dissolving into a swirling vortex of dread. The scream came again, sharper, more desperate, pulling him inexorably from the safety of his room.

He stumbled out of bed, his bare feet hitting the cold wooden floor. He didn't bother with slippers, and didn't waste a second on a single thought. The urgency in his mother's cries propelled him forward, a primal instinct overriding all reason. He bolted down the stairs, the aged wood groaning under his weight, each step echoing the frantic rhythm of his pulse.

The kitchen was bathed in the dim, pre-dawn light filtering through the window. A half-eaten apple lay on the counter, a testament to the normalcy that had reigned just hours before. Now, the air was thick with a palpable sense of wrongness, a silent scream that amplified the one tearing through the morning air. He burst through the back door and into the garden.

The scene that unfolded before him was a macabre tableau painted in shades of horror. His mother was on the ground, writhing in agony, her body contorted in unnatural angles. The meticulously arranged flowerbeds, once a source of pride and joy, were now trampled and marred, mirroring the chaos consuming her. But it was the dark, crimson pool spreading beneath her that stole the air from his lungs. Blood. So much blood.

His heart skipped a beat, then stuttered, threatening to cease altogether. He moved towards her, each step heavy, leaden with dread. As he drew closer, his mother struggled to her knees, her face a mask of unimaginable pain. Her eyes, usually warm and filled with affection, were wide with fear and a desperate plea for help he didn't understand.

With trembling hands, she ripped at the front of her dress, the fabric tearing with a sickening sound. Elias gasped. Dangling from her collarbone, a flap of skin hung loose, detached, almost as if it was peeling away from the underlying flesh. It was pale, translucent, and disturbingly unnatural.

She reached out to him, her hand outstretched, a silent supplication. "Elias," she croaked, her voice a strained whisper, barely audible above the frantic pounding in his ears. "Help me…"

He didn't hesitate. He reached out and took her hand, his fingers wrapping around hers. But the moment his skin made contact, a wave of nausea washed over him. He felt a strange, unsettling texture, like grasping something not quite solid, something…wrong.

Then, with horrifying slowness, the skin from her hand and wrist began to peel away, separating from the flesh beneath as if it were nothing more than a discarded glove. It slid off, leaving behind a raw, pulpy mass of muscle and bone, glistening in the pale morning light.

His mother screamed again, a piercing shriek of pure, unadulterated agony that echoed through the garden. The sound was so intense, so visceral, that it felt like a physical blow, sending shards of ice through his veins.

Elias recoiled, stumbling backward, his eyes fixed on the grotesque spectacle unfolding before him. He stared at the detached skin in his hand, the texture chillingly alien, the color a sickly, unnatural pallor. It felt cold, clammy, and utterly devoid of life.

His mind struggled to comprehend what he was witnessing. This couldn't be real. This had to be a nightmare, a grotesque figment of his imagination. But the blood, the pain, the sheer, overwhelming horror of the scene screamed its reality into his soul.

He dropped the skin as if it were burning him. It landed on the stone patio with a soft, sickening thud. His mother continued to scream, her body convulsing, more skin peeling away from her arms, revealing the raw, bloody flesh beneath.

He wanted to help her, to comfort her, to somehow stop the agonizing transformation that was consuming her. But he was paralyzed by fear, frozen in place by the sheer, unadulterated horror of the situation.

The air grew heavy, thick with an oppressive sense of dread. The birds, which had been chirping merrily just moments before, fell silent. The garden, once a sanctuary of peace and tranquility, now felt like a stage for a macabre performance, a nightmare unfolding in excruciating detail.

As his mother's screams began to heighten in volume, he saw the skin from her lips and cheeks rip and fall off her face, until it was only a red mass with bulging eyes and hair.

Elias wanted to run, to escape the horrific scene playing out before him. But he couldn't. He was rooted to the spot, held captive by a morbid fascination, a horrifying compulsion to witness the completion of this grotesque metamorphosis.

He watched, helpless and horrified, as the last vestiges of his mother's skin peeled away, revealing the raw, bloody, and unrecognizable creature beneath.

Then suddenly she ceased , falling backwards onto the cold floor , drowning in a pool of her own flesh and blood. What was left of her face displayed a look of absolute terror.

Elias could not even let himself feel grief , he was filled with terror. This must be the work of the fruit , the same fruit he had given to her and eaten himself. Was he to have the same fate as his mother? What will the other villagers think when they come across this scene?

As he tried to pick up what was left of his loving mother so that he could bury her he decided at least to give the cursed fruit a name ~ 'The flaying fruit , Hesperidium of death'

He survived, every moment of his life regretting giving his only parent the mysterious cursed fruit out of ignorance, he regretted that she was not in the warmth of his arms when she was dying in agony.

Elias survived the fruit , but not his grief.

He chose to hang from the tree that had killed his mother. His lifeless swaying body was a warning sign to all those that crossed its treacherous path. He swung slowly rotting into carrion flesh that no bird dared to eat.

As weeks went by the tree branches intertwined with the bones and remains of flesh that were left behind on Elias's body , slowly pulling him backwards towards the tree's stem , when fruits fell from the tree they landed on his skeleton encased in branches and bone.

Flaying~

The word "flaying" refers to the act of removing skin, either from an animal or a person.

Flaying of humans is used as a method of torture or execution, depending on how much of the skin is removed. This is often referred to as flaying alive. There are also records of people flayed after death, generally as a means of debasing the corpse of a prominent enemy or criminal, sometimes related to religious beliefs (e.g., to deny an afterlife); sometimes the skin is used, again for deterrence, esoteric/ritualistic purposes, etc.

'The Flaying of Saint Bartholomew'

'Michelangelo's The Last Judgment' - St Bartholomew holding the knife of his martyrdom and his flayed skin; it is conjectured that Michelangelo included a self-portrait depicting himself as St Bartholomew after he had been flayed alive.

'Apollo flaying Marsyas' attributed to Giovanni Bilivert

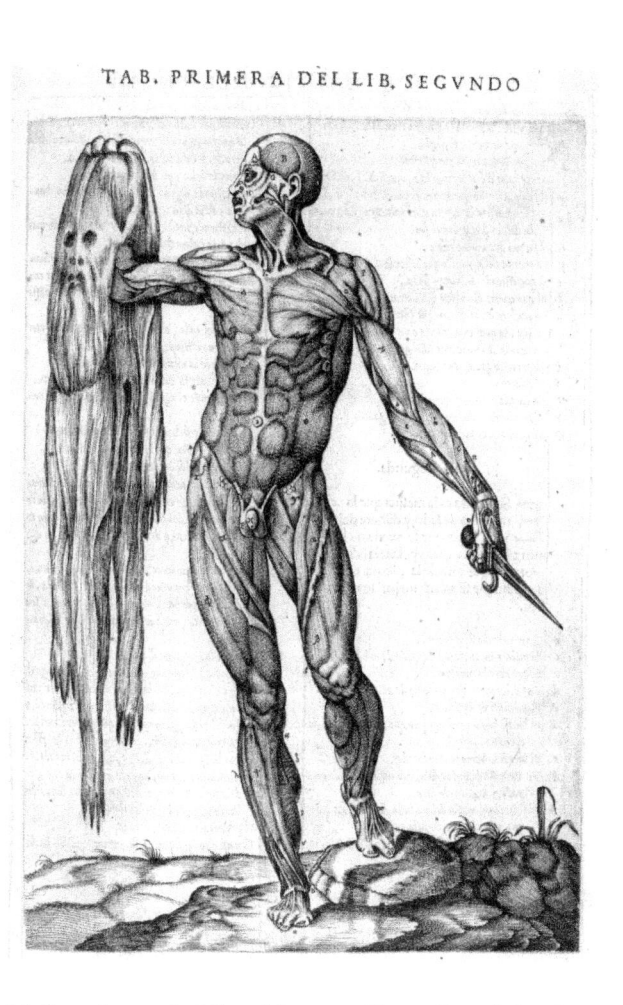

'A flayed man holding his own skin ~ Royal Academy of Arts'

Printed in Dunstable, United Kingdom